The Healthy Wolf

For Jonathan and Angela for
teaching me winning ways.
~DB

For Andrew, Robert and Elizabeth. x
~MS

MYRIAD BOOKS LIMITED
35 Bishopsthorpe Road, London SE26 4PA

First published in 2002 by
Magi Publications
1 The Coda Centre, 189 Munster Road, London SW6 6AW

Text © 2002 David Bedford
Illustrations © 2002 Mandy Stanley
David Bedford and Mandy Stanley have asserted their rights
to be identified as the author and illustrator of this work
under the Copyright, Designs and Patents Act, 1988.

ISBN 1 905 161 88 3

Printed in China

The Healthy Wolf

David Bedford

Illustrated by Mandy Stanley

MYRIAD
BOOKS LIMITED

Wilfred was a greedy young wolf who liked
all the wrong foods . . .
Tangy, crunchy smoky-bacon crisps.

Mm! Mmmmmm!

Sweet, chewy chocolate bars.

Aaahh!

All washed down with lots of sugary, fizzy drinks.

Yum!

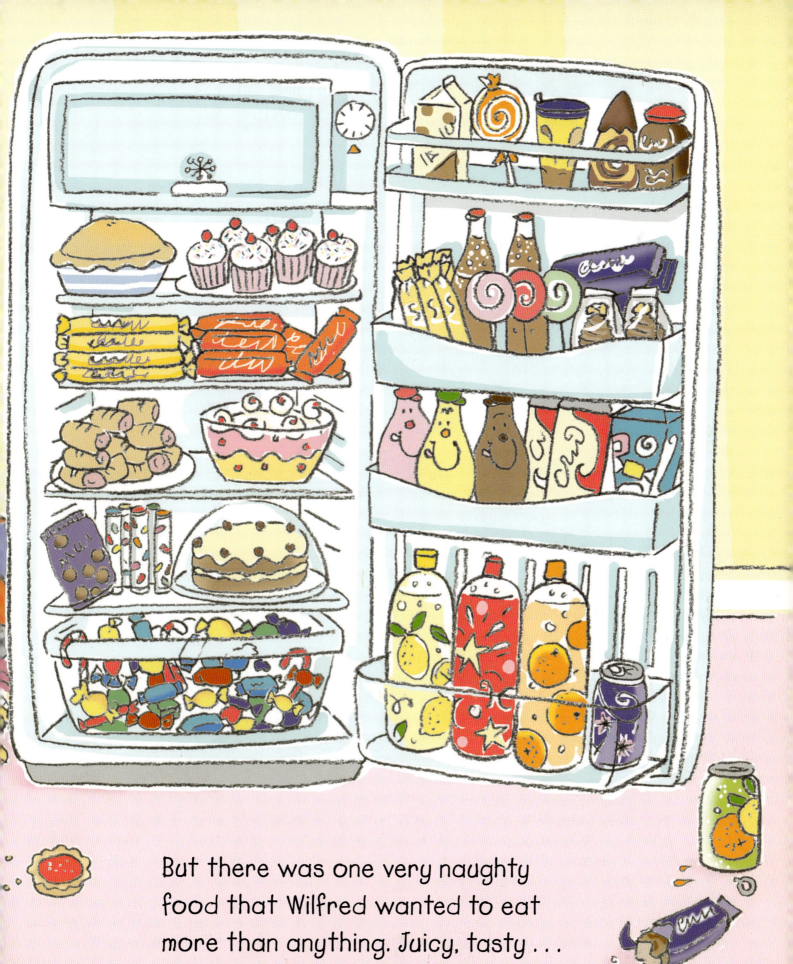

But there was one very naughty
food that Wilfred wanted to eat
more than anything. Juicy, tasty . . .

CHILDREN!

But he never did. After years of eating crisps and chocolate bars, Wilfred was very unhealthy, and much too slow to catch any.

As the years went by Wilfred
grew more and more unhealthy.

It got so bad that his teeth were
too rotten to chew anything.

By the time he was ten the only food he could eat was icky sticky porridge! Yuk! Then one day, his diet changed forever . . .

The Brownbread family all thought
Wilfred looked hilarious when they first met him.
"Look at that silly old wolf with porridge on his chin,"
laughed Octavia. "He couldn't scare a flea!"

But Mrs Brownbread felt a bit sorry for him.
"Don't laugh," she said. "Let's take him home
with us and *make him better*."

Fortunately, Mr Brownbread was a dentist, so Wilfred got his teeth fixed for free. Unfortunately, they were all rotten and needed pulling out!

Then he gave Wilfred new fangs made out of hard plastic. "From now on you must brush your teeth three times a day, and eat plenty of fresh fruit. Look at me, I'm full of fruit," said Mr Brownbread.

"Then you must be very good for my teeth!" said Wilfred, as he lunged to gobble up Mr Brownbread.

SNAP!

SNAP!

SNAP!

But Mr Brownbread
was too quick. He was up an
apple tree, raining apples
down on Wilfred before he
could so much as sniff at him!

Next Wilfred went to see
Mrs Brownbread . . .

As a doctor she was horrified when she saw what he'd been eating all these years!
"You are extremely unhealthy, and from now on you must only eat good foods, like me. I'm full of good foods."

"Okay, then!" said Wilfred, "If that's what the doctor has ordered." And he lunged to gobble up Mrs Brownbread.

SNAP! SNAP!

But Mrs Brownbread was too quick.
She hid in a cupboard before
he could take one bite!

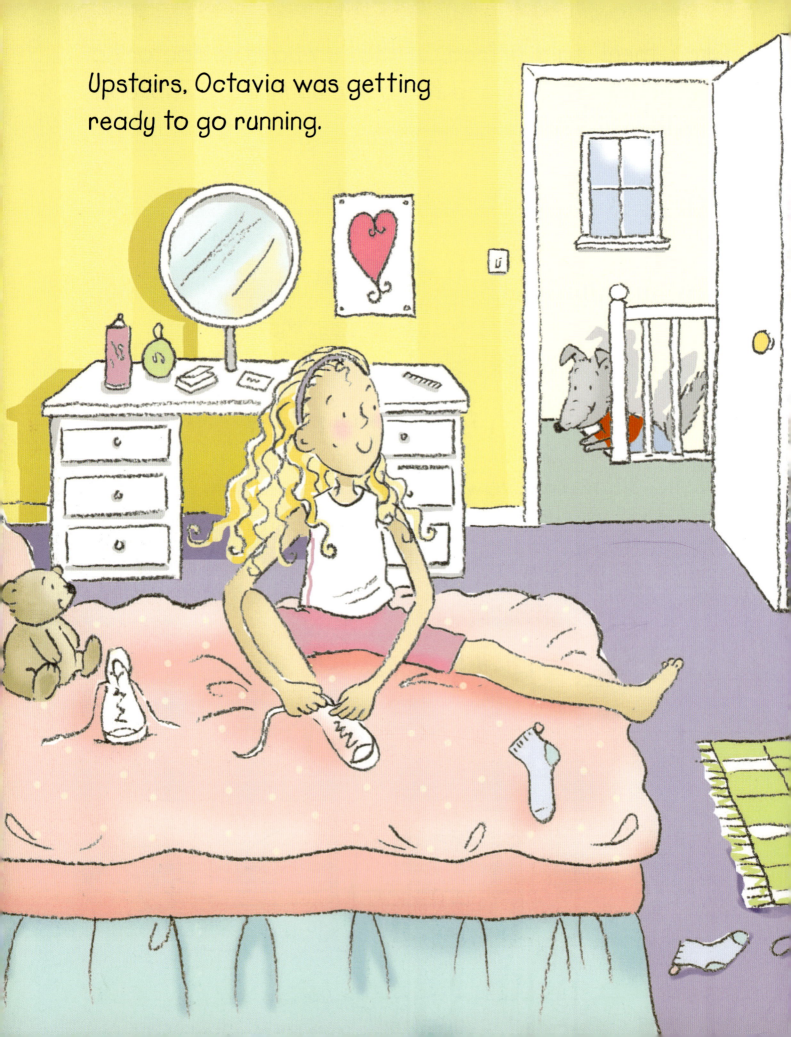

Upstairs, Octavia was getting ready to go running.

"Would you like to come running with me?" asked Octavia.
"If you run every day you'll soon be fit and healthy like
the rest of us."
"No thanks!" said Wilfred, "I'm not allowed fast food,
so you'd better stay right where you are!"
And he lunged straight for her . . .

Unfortunately, she was very good at running.

"You're even sillier than you look," she laughed.

Wilfred was fed up that everyone else was too quick for him. He was determined to catch them. Every day for a whole week he ate . . .

Apples for breakfast.

Mm! Mmmmm!

Bananas for lunch.

Aaahh!

And soup for tea.

Yum!

After each meal he brushed his fangs
until the sharp points sparkled.

And every day he went out running with Octavia.

Each day, he got nearer . . .

and nearer . . .

and **nearer,**

until...

He'd had so much fun that
week that he'd forgotten all about
eating her, and just wanted to beat her!

Three cheers for Wilfred, the healthy wolf!